Chapter 1-The Calm before the Storm

Charlie's head throbbed as she woke up violently from her dream. For a very split second she couldn't remember who she was or where she was. Looking around she found five sleeping children all in sleeping bags with bits of popcorn and crisps around their mouths. As her memory came back, she noticed that one sleeping bag was empty. Her memory still hazy, she walked out onto the balcony to be greeted by someone she knew. As her memory came rushing back, she realized that he was Michael, one of her closest friends from when they were younger. "So, what are you doing out here?" Charlie asked as from his demeanour, he seemed to have been out here for quite a long time. "Could ask you the same thing" he said chuckling to himself. Charlie knew from his face that he was out here for a reason, but she couldn't help not asking him. "So, how's life going for you?" Charlie asked desperate to continue the conversation. "It's going fine yeah, my Dad just opened up another restaurant"

"Oh really?" Charlie asked, excitement filling her eyes. Charlie loved being treated like a V.I.P whenever she and Michael went to one of his

Dad's restaurants. Michael not so much. "Well best I get back to bed" Michael said. "Tomorrow is another day."

"Charlie, CHARLIE" She jolted up in a rushed manner. "Are you ok?" She looked up to the voice of Gabriel, one of Charlie's friends. At first, she didn't understand what was happening but when she looked to see everyone dressed and ready to go, she realised that she'd slept in. "Oh, damn it" She screamed as she hurried out of bed apologising profusely to Michael's parents ,however something bothered her. Michael's dad looked odd, emptier than his usual self. 'Never mind that' she thought to herself exiting the house and into the car. She decided to doze off in the car as Freddy's was quite far from where Michael lived. As she fell asleep, she heard the commotion of what else was happening inside the car.

"Hey give it back Fritz it's mine" Cassidy shrieked as Fritz had a hold of her phone and was holding it up in the air. It was like Fritz to do these kinds of things as he was considered the 'bad boy' of the group. Many people questioned why he hung around them but the rest didn't mind. As for the others, Gabriel was very popular at their school, it seemed like everyone liked him so he tried to find people that liked him for his personality and not his looks. Michael was the typical no interests, no features that you would see in a lot of harem anime. Then there was Cassidy who was usually very shy most of the time. Susie was the airhead but pretty one. Jeremy was that self-centred egotistical boy that you seem to find in almost every school and Charlie was just Charlie, everyone always said. It was pretty shocking to see all these different people come together and be really good friends.

"Ha, try and take it from me" Fritz jokingly said before handing it back to Cassidy. "You kids seem energetic today" Michael's dad said. The way he said it really creeped Charlie out, but Michael didn't seem to mind so she didn't question it. At last they finally got to the restaurant to Susie's excited screams. "Oh my god shut up Susie!" shouted Fritz as they all got out of the car. "Do we really have to come here?" Cassidy timidly asked. "Of course," said Jeremy "I wouldn't want people not seeing me"

"Shut up" Gabriel said before jokingly hitting Jeremy round the head. It was clear to everyone that Jeremy was jealous of Gabriel's popularity but he didn't let that get in the way of their friendship, even if he liked to pretend that he was the best looking one. Since Michael's dad owned the restaurant, they got seated in a special room only really meant for kids with birthdays. After about an hour of eating pizza and chatting Charlie left to go to the toilet. As she left, she saw one of the mascots walking around; this was normal as they would usually come round to get orders but behind him were a line of kids looking happy. As she watched she saw that they were heading into a back room with a sign that said 'Employees only' written on it. Curious, she followed them and peeked through the door, there was no one there. Not even the bunny was there just faint specs of blood on the floor. 'OH MY' she thought running back to the room of the party looking pale and cold. "What's wrong?" Gabriel asked before Michael's dad ran into the room "We need to leave!" He said, panicked. Suddenly they heard crying and screaming from outside. Without looking all the kids ran out of the building to the car and Michael's dad drove off in a hurry.

Chapter 2-The aftermath Of the Storm

No one did or said anything on the way back. The usually cynical Fritz was quiet and shaking with fear. The shy Cassidy looked terrified now. Everyone was on edge now after what just happened. It seemed that Charlie was hit the most by this. She never turned up to the meeting spot for her friends and she started doing worse in school. Many teachers tried talking to her but to no avail. "We got to do something" said Fritz.

"Like what? Gabriel said "We can't do anything if she doesn't want to."

Just then Cassidy started walking over to Charlie. "Hey Cassidy where are you going?" Fritz asked but Cassidy ignored him.

"Charlie, are you ok?" Cassidy asked in her typical shy and quiet way.

"Go away Cassidy" Charlie shouted. "I asked if you were ok" Cassidy also shouted with a confidence that no one had ever seen before. Charlie looked up shocked to see Cassidy like this. Charlie attempted to get up and grab her bag but was stopped by Cassidy who grabbed her hand and said "Charlie, this isn't right, you should be confiding in your friends, if you spend the rest of your days alone then you'll never heal so please Charlie, come back to us."

Everyone around had their mouths open in shock at what happened, except Fritz who smiled and muttered "so you've finally shown your true colours to everyone"

Charlie stared blindly at Cassidy, lost for words. "Cassidy, I..."

"Just come back to your friends Charlie, we know you better than anyone. We were all scared that day, we were oblivious to anything that happened so don't go blaming yourself or anyone else for what happened."

"But it was someone's fault!" Charlie said. "It was the bunny's fault. I saw him lead the victims into the back room; all of this is his fault and someday I will find him!"

Chapter 3

Cassidy went home that night wondering what happened to her. She had never been like that before. The only person that she's ever done that too is Fritz. She felt confidant but also nervous and shy. When she got home, she got a text from Fritz.

'Well done today, you may not feel like it but you did great' it read.

Even though she felt more confident after hearing that from Fritz she still felt like that wasn't her. 'Oh well' she thought laying into bed. 'At least I can look forward to my brother's drama performance later today'

The next day as she woke up her brother Aiden started shouting in her face. "It's my performance today Cass are you going to see it, are you?"

She had gotten used to Aiden's hyperactivity so she just said "Yeah, I mean I have to"

Aiden seemed to have lost all his energy when she said that so she just went downstairs to have breakfast.

On the way to school she ran into Fritz who rarely ever walked.

"Oh, hey Cass" he said "Want to walk together?"

"Oh, um sure" she muttered as they continued walking.

School went by like every other day but to Cassidy it didn't feel like it, people started whispering whenever she walked by anyone. They only stopped thanks to Fritz threatening them.

"Man don't people talk about anything other than random stuff that has nothing to do with them" Fritz said as they walked to the usual hang out spot where they meet the others.

"Oh, hey guys!" said Michael as they arrived.

"Hey!" said Fritz.

They all talked for a bit before heading home. "Wait, stay here Cassidy" said Fritz as everyone was heading home. "W...why?" Cassidy asked

"Because I want to help you" replied Fritz. "Help me?" repeated Cassidy looking confused. "Yes, that's what I said, help you."

"Help me with what?" Cassidy asked. "I want to help you get more confident!"

"Wh...What?" Yelled Cassidy.

"Well you seem to be getting better by second" said Fritz in his usual snarky way.

"That's not what I meant!" said Cassidy but Fritz's face turned serious.

"Listen, you need this. You can't go through life just taking other people's crap; you got to learn to stand up for yourself. I saw you do it, with Charlie yesterday so I know it's possible for you to learn."

Cassidy was lost for words. "See, now you understand" Fritz remarked, jumping closer to Cassidy and smiling.

"Well, I guess its ok" Cassidy whispered.

"COME ON, I know you can be louder than that" Fritz shouted.

"Ok then! From now on I'll work hard to be more confident and to always stand up for myself! Just like you always has been Fritz"

Fritz looked surprised then looked down sad. "Yeah... always have been"

Chapter 4-2 weeks before Fritz joined

"Fritz... FRITZ!" It was his brother. "Wake up, Mom and Dad want us down for breakfast."

Fritz realising, he slept in jumped up out of bed and started rushing around his room getting his clothes on.

Downstairs, Fritz and his family started eating breakfast. "So, Fritz." His mum said suddenly. "Your report card came in. It was alright but I saw you got a 1 on social skills."

'Yeah but mum you shouldn't care about that I got really good grades on all my other subjects' Fritz thought angrily.

"Yeah but...but...ok mum I'll try better next time" the words couldn't escape him.

It seemed to Fritz that he was a nobody everywhere he went. At school everyone avoided him like the plague, except for one group of people who always looked at everyone else, rolled their eyes and went back to what they were doing.

One day, Fritz was just sitting down when a girl came up to him whom he had never seen before.

"Um...hi" she said to him.

Fritz, thinking it was another prank by the popular kids responded with "Oh, um...hi listen if Dave and the others asked you to do this then can you go away please"

"What, you mean those clowns. No, me and my friends over there thought you were a bit lonely." Fritz turned to see a group of people standing there watching.

"Um... thanks I'll see what your friend group is like."

"Rude" the girl said out of the blue

"Um... anyway what's your name?" Fritz asked trying to sound as polite as possible.

"You go first!" she said smirking at him.

"Oh me?" Fritz stumbled confused about this girl's demeanour. "It's Fritz"

"What a dumb name!" she retorted. "Mine's Stephanie"

The kids in Stephanie's friend group looked much older than he was. It was kind of intimidating how he looked the youngest one there; even Stephanie now looked older than he was.

"Hey Steph, who's the new kid?" one of the guys asked.

"Oh him, he looked lonely on the bench so I thought he could come here" replied Stephanie.

The guys all looked at Fritz with glaring eyes that made Fritz want to run away.

"But guys listen…" She took them off to the side and was talking to them. When they came back, they walked up to him with smiles on their faces. "Welcome to the ga- I mean friend group!"

Everything about this seemed so odd to Fritz. He looked on his phone when he got back home and he had been added to a group chat with Stephanie and those other guys. He didn't know how they got his number. All of this seemed really suspicious to him.

At school the next day. There was a lot of talk about some guy at our school getting robbed yesterday by a group of people. Fritz took no notice of it as he was used to the rumours that usually spread around school. When suddenly, his phone buzzed. He looked at the message, it was from Stephanie.

"Hey, can you meet us at the school gate after school?" it read.

'Why would she text me that?' he thought. However, curiosity got the better of him so he decided to go.

Stephanie's whole demeanour had changed. Her hands were fidgeting and she had a look of worry and panic on her face.

"What's wrong?" Fritz asked. Then, he noticed the other guys she was with looking at her with a sense of rage.

"Give us our money back Steph!" he roared. Looking over at them, they were all stumbling around looking drowsy. 'Are they drunk? How old are they?' Fritz thought.

They started getting closer to Stephanie.

'Crap, I've got to do something' he thought.

Without thinking he stepped in front of Stephanie.

"Go Steph run!" he shouted before she got up and started running.

"Oh, that was your last mistake kid!" one of the guys shouted.

For some reason, Fritz wasn't feeling dread or worry or anything. His only thought was

'I've got to give Stephanie time to get away!'

When he came back to his senses, he was in a strange room. It was mostly white and blue with a brown door. He had a breathing device on and wires attached to him. He then realized that it was a hospital.

"You've been out for quite a while" a voice said. It was the nurse. "You gave your family quite a shock" he added.

Sitting up Fritz finally came back to reality. "Where are they doctor?"

"In the waiting room, I can bring them in if you want." He replied.

"Yes please" said Fritz.

The doctor dropped what he was doing and went through the door that led to the room. When he came back his parents, his brother and Stephanie were there with him.

Chapter 5

Gabriel always viewed himself as just an ordinary kid with no aspirations or goals in life. He had no idea that he would have become the most popular guy at school just by existing. He only wanted to make one or two friends while he was in school but something odd to him happened. He saw Jeremy sitting on the floor reading his book but he felt drawn to him like a moth to a light. At first, he just thought that he just wanted to be kind to a kid that looked lonely. Then he started talking to other kids and they all talked like they'd known each other for a long time.

Then when they went to Freddy's and that incident happened it all felt like they needed to be there. It felt as if they were supposed to go there.

He had heard that a guy named Fritz came out of hospital and he felt as though he should talk to him. To his surprise, everyone else felt like they should and Fritz himself even felt like he had to.

One night, Gabriel dreamt that a strange person was talking to him.

"Gabriel, you must listen. You and your friends are special, you are vital to the re-construction of this plane of existence." It said.

Talking to his friends the next day, Gabriel was surprised that they had the exact same dream as him.

"What could this mean?" Susie asked. Looking over, Gabriel could see Michael fidgeting about as if he was uncomfortable.

"Something you want to say Michael?" Gabriel asked him.

"N...No" Michael said in response.

"Anyway, it's probably just a coincidence!" Michael added.

"Yeah maybe" replied Charlie.

"Besides, it's getting late, we should all head home" Michael said

Charlie had never seen Michael like this but she chose to ignore it.

When Gabriel got home, he suddenly felt really tired. It was quite late so it made sense to him.

That night, he had another strange dream. He found himself in a dark and dank room. The floor was full of moss and insects. There were multiple workbenches with various tools of knives and scissors. Gabriel was there for about 3 minutes before two figures came in wearing all black and hoods over their heads disguising their faces. One was way shorter than the other and Gabriel couldn't hear their conversation but he heard some of it.

"So, they're the ones I'm after! You better make sure that Charlie and her friends come to me! So, what's your plan?"

Gabriel woke up with a jolt panting and sweating.

'What the hell was that?' Gabriel thought. 'Was it just another dream? If not, who or what is after us?'

At school, Gabriel told everyone about his dream thinking that they'd say it was just another dream, but they told him they all had the exact same dream in the exact same way.

"This can't be a coincidence!" Susie exclaimed.

"I'm sure it is" Michael replied. "I mean, why would someone come after us?"

"Fine, let's just go home" Jeremy said after a while.

Chapter 6

When Charlie got home, she went up to her room to think about what had happened over the last couple of days. However, when she went to pick up her water bottle, she saw that it was levitating in mid-air. Startled, she jumped back and the bottle fell on the floor.

'I must be losing my mind' she thought going back to pick it up. However, the same thing happened. The water bottle levitated in her room before travelling into her hand.

"Dad!" she shouted out. Charlie's dad responded by coming into the room.

"Yeah Charlie?" he asked.

Charlie dropped the water bottle and went to pick it up again. The same thing happened where it levitated in the room for a few moments before going into her hand.

Charlie's dad's face went from concerned to of complete and utter worry.

"Oh no, it's happened. I didn't think it would now." Charlie's Dad said. "Tell me Charlie, what have been your dreams lately?"

"Um...well. There was one where someone told me that I and my friends were special and then there was one where a man said that he was after us!"

"Oh no, it's already happened."

'Then it's true then' Charlie thought

"Charlie don't leave this room; I need to do something" Charlie's dad said.

While waiting for her dad to come back, Charlie went on her phone to tell the others what just happened. However, relatively the same thing happened to others.

When Charlie's dad came back, he knelt down and said

"Charlie, I know this might sound crazy, but one of your friends told the man in black about you."

This shook Charlie and she thought she was going to cry.

"W…what do you mean?"

"Charlie, we need to separate you from your friends for a while. One of them isn't really your friend but we don't know who. So, to do this, we need to move!"

'Move?' Charlie thought.

"It will take me a couple weeks to be able to get another house"

"Dad, Am I going to be ok?" Charlie asked.

Charlie's dad responded by pulling Charlie into a tight embrace.

"It's ok Charlie; you're going to be just fine."

Chapter 7-departure

"So, I guess this is goodbye" Charlie said to everyone.

"Don't say that" Fritz replied. "I'm sure we will see each other soon."

"Goodbye Charlie" Cassidy said.

"Hope we see you again" said Gabriel

"G...goodbye Charlie" said Michael with his head down.

"I'm 100% sure we'll see each other again" Susie exclaimed.

"You'd better come back" Jeremy said.

Charlie walked towards her dad's car looking into the horizon at a future that was yet to come.

Part 2

Chapter 1

Leaning over the coffin, a single tear fell from Charlie's eyes as she placed her hand on it in remembrance, her father's coffin.

The scenery was all dull and boring, rain pouring down, hiding the tears of the people there. Charlie hardly recognised any of the people there. To her, nothing seemed right about all of this.

'How could he have died so young?' she thought to herself. It was like her whole world shattered right there and then.

Even after the ceremony, she stayed to look at the grave when her aunt Carole walked up to her.

"Oh, your father was a great man" She said but acted as though she didn't mean it.

"Yeah, he was" Charlie replied.

"Although, when I saw him, he spent too much time on his work than on his family" she retorted.

"Well, I think that he spent as much time as I needed with me" Charlie then remarked.

Aunt Carole scowled at her and then walked off.

'Maybe dad wasn't as popular as I'd like to believe' Charlie thought to herself.

As she got up to head home, her phone buzzed. Looking at it, she saw that it was from Michael, it read

"Hi Charlie, I know all of us haven't spoken in a while, but I think we should all see each other again"

Charlie used to beg her dad to let her go back but he always said no. So, she replied with

"Sure, have the others agreed?"

Michael then responded with

"Yeah, so let's say 8pm tonight"

"Sure"

Getting to her car, she couldn't help but feel a sense excitement but also nervousness.

'You aren't a kid anymore' she thought to herself.

It had been 10 years since she'd moved and throughout those 10 years, she'd been desperate to go back to her old town to see all her friends again, but for some reason, Charlie's dad never let her go back. Every time she asked him, he would look very nervous and say

"Maybe next time"

Arriving back in town was a nostalgia trip for Charlie. Play areas she and her friends would play at all the time, her old school that still had lessons going on, restaurants that could make any child happy.

Checking her watch, she saw that she was still quite early so she decided to go to her old house not too far away from where she was then.

Charlie's dad was hoping to make some money selling the house, but no one wanted to buy it so he gave up.

Looking at it now, she could tell why nobody wanted it. The door was falling off, the windows looked like they were going to shatter, and the whole of the outside was filled with moss and insect nests.

The inside wasn't much better either, the wallpaper was peeling off, furniture was worn and ripped and all the other doors in the house were covered with moss.

Charlie decided to go into her dad's old office to see what exactly he hid in there. Opening the door, she thought she saw her dad at his chair on his computer, but he disappeared within a split second.

All the drawers in the desk were out and paper had been scattered all across the floor with various equations and maths principles on it.

Charlie's father used to be a math teacher before he started a business with one of his best friends. His business was then bought out by Michael's dad and that's when they met.

Checking her watch again, she saw that she should probably leave to go meet everyone.

Looking back at the house she waved goodbye and thought she saw her father waving back at her.

While Charlie was on the road again, she saw her favourite restaurant on the way, the one they went to for Gabriel's party 10 years ago. However, like Charlie's house it was closed and decaying so she decided to visit it one last time since the diner they were meeting at was right next to it.

Parking her car in the diner carpark, she snuck round to the restaurant to say one final goodbye. However, when she got there, she was surprised to see two people already there talking to each other.

"Um... hello, who are you?" Charlie called out to them.

"Hm, oh Charlie, hey how's it been going" one of the guys said.

Looking confused, the other person spoke

"Do you not recognise us?"

"Come on Charlie, it's us Gabriel and Jeremy"

Hit with a sudden realisation, Charlie said

"Oh right, sorry about that"

Both Jeremy and Gabriel looked like completely different people to how they did when he was younger. Jeremy now looked like a typical Hollywood actor compared to his scruffy, dirty look he had when he was younger. His voice had a smooth suave tone that sounded kind of British. Gabriel on the other hand, looked just like a regular person, not too good looking, his voice felt quite flat or monotone.

"So, what are you guys doing here?" Charlie asked.

"We were just seeing how this place looked after all these years. Doesn't really look well does it?" Gabriel replied.

"To think, that so much happened within these doors" Jeremy added.

"Yeah I guess your right" Charlie said looking up at the giant sign that towered over all the other buildings in the area.

Touching the walls, she felt the age that came with the place and she felt the history of it, all the good and all the bad.

Finally, Gabriel snapped her out of it.

"Holy, we got to get moving" He shouted.

"Ah yes, we should" Jeremy responded.

Walking up to the restaurant, the three of them could see that there was quite a lot of people in the diner.

"We seem to be late" Jeremy retorted.

"Yeah, we can see that Jeremy" Gabriel said sarcastically.

They walked inside and the waiter asked

"Do you have a reservation?"

Just as Charlie was about to respond someone shouted:

"CHARLIE!"

Michael then came up and told the waiter that they were with him.

Sitting around the table, it felt to Charlie that she had never left in the first place.

"So how's it been Charlie?" Fritz asked.

"Yeah I've been good"

Fritz sounded and looked the exact same as he did when he was younger which made Charlie smile a little.

"You remember Cassidy don't you Charlie" Fritz asked gesturing to the corner of the table to where Cassidy was.

Cassidy looked completely different to when they were younger. Her hair was longer and she was a lot taller than everyone else.

She wasn't focusing on anyone in the room, instead she was staring out the window so Charlie decided to break her out it.

"Hey Cassidy" Charlie said. Suddenly, Cassidy jolted up and turned to face Charlie.

"Huh, oh my gosh I'm so sorry… wait is that you Charlie?" Cassidy asked.

"Yep it sure is" laughed Fritz.

"Wait, where's Susie?" Charlie asked Michael.

Michael looked down before saying

"Well, that's why I brought you guys here. Susie is dead"

The news hit everyone like a train.

"Dead, no… no she can't be!" Gabriel said stumbling back against a wall

"It is true unfortunately" Michael replied

Nobody moved for a while after that. Not until the waiter came round to take orders from everyone.

They had to make it look like everything was fine so that they wouldn't disturb the people around them.

Dinner was extremely awkward, barely anyone talked throughout.

"Well guess I'd better get going" said Fritz.

Just then Charlie felt a sharp pain to her neck and she was out cold.

Chapter 2

Charlie awoke in a strange room with dim candles filling the room. She could feel a sense of familiarity with it but couldn't figure out why. She could see a table in front of her and she soon realized that she was tied up.

'Where am I?' she thought to herself.

Just then, she heard a door open behind her then shut and a masked man came round the table in front of her and stared.

"Who are you?" she asked.

"Oh, how sad" he responded. "With this mask on you don't know who I am but if I took it off you'd know exactly who I was" He laughed cynically.

"And what's that supposed to mean?" Charlie retorted still confused on where she was.

Suddenly the man grabbed Charlie's neck.

"Listen you, I could kill you right here and now, but I'm not going to because I need something from you" He shouted.

"What do you need?" Charlie asked him.

"I need your powers" The masked man said

Charlie let out a laugh

"My...powers? Are you drunk by any chance?" Charlie jokingly asked.

"Don't play dumb with me!" He shouted punching a wall.

"Just who are you anyway?" She asked

The man was masked but Charlie could tell that he was smirking underneath.

'How could she do that?' she asked herself in her head

"Trust me, if I took off this mask you'd know everything about me. Just like how I know everything about you" he laughed sadistically.

"What do you mean?" Charlie asked.

"I'm someone very close to you let's say"
He grinned.

"What do you mean by that?" Charlie asked

"Stop asking me QUESTIONS!" He shouted throwing away the table and hitting Charlie in the stomach.

"Now, are you going to give me your powers or not?" he asked.

"What powers?" Charlie asked frustrated.

"Fine then, if you aren't going to talk I'll make you talk"

Charlie was out cold.

When she came to she was in another dirty and dark room. It looked like a prison cell.

It was a prison cell.

'Where am I?' she wondered

She heard a voice

"Psst, Charlie, you there?" It was Fritz.

"Fritz? Where are you?" Charlie asked in a daze.

"I'm in the cell next to you" Fritz replied

Charlie looked over at the bars that were separating the two cells and limped over. Inside was Fritz and all her other friends.

"Ok guys Charlie's up. Jeremy do your thing" Fritz said.

Jeremy stood up and put his hands together.

Suddenly, the floor started to rumble and shots of what looked like tree branches shot up from beneath the floor crushing the wall giving them an escape route.

"Ok, let's go guys" Fritz called.

Everyone got on their feet ready to move.

"Wait hold on, what's going on, first I get interrogated by some masked guy, then this happens, what is going on?" Charlie asked

"You seriously don't know?" Gabriel questioned before Fritz cut him off.

"Never mind now we'll explain on the way" said Fritz.

"Wait, where's Michael?" Cassidy asked

"Crap, where is he?" Fritz panicked.

"Don't worry, we'll find him on the way"
Said Gabriel.

"Ok fine then. Jeremy break down Charlie's
door so we can get going"

"Right"

And so, they were off trying to find Michael.

Chapter 3

"There he is!" Cassidy shouted.

They stopped in front of Michael.

"What are you doing out here?" Fritz asked Michael

"I managed to escape, sorry I left you behind. I was going to come back I swear" Michael replied.

"Well, at least we're all safe now" Jeremy said smirking at Gabriel.

"Now, tell me what is going on?" Charlie asked.

"Ok, fine" said Fritz.

"Remember when you had that dream when you were little about that guy who said that we were the key to saving earth?"

"Yeah, but wasn't that just a dream?" Charlie asked.

"No it wasn't, it was a celestial being telling us the truth. Our parents knew it because we were chosen to hold special powers to help maintain peace on earth. So, our parents taught us how to use our powers. However, judging by your reaction, I'm guessing your father never taught you how to control yours."

"Well, maybe but what powers do I have? What powers to you guys have?" Charlie asked

"Well, Jeremy has the power of nature and the earth, I have fire, Cassidy has water, Gabriel has lightning and I don't know what you or Michael have. Are you happy now?" Fritz asked.

"Wait, Can you guys teach me how to get mine" Charlie asked

They all smiled to each other.

"Ok sure" said Gabriel.

"So how did you guys unlock yours?" Charlie asked.

"Well, you have to have a near death experience, then your powers will help you get out of it and the-"

"CHARLIE!" She heard a voice from inside her head.

"Charlie, one of your friends is not who they say they are. Please Charlie, I don't know who it is but that man in the mask, he is one of them. He doesn't have powers like the rest so gather all your friends that have proven that they have powers and run. Charlie please, get to safety"

It was her Dad.

She stumbled back, the rest hurried around her to see what was wrong.

"Charlie, run!" Her Dad said in her mind.

"Everyone, prove to me that you have these powers that you say you do.

"Charlie, we've run out of energy what do you mean?" Fritz asked confused.

Charlie just like magic figured out what to do next. She group huddled everyone and showed them what she saw.

"Listen, let's not be too hasty. We now know what Charlie's powers are so we should stick together and as soon as someone acts suspicious we'll have Charlie figure them out" Gabriel suggested.

"Right" everyone said.

Suddenly, there was a buzzing noise. It was coming from Michael's phone.

"Hello" he said into it.

"Oh my…" he said covering his mouth

"Yes thank you officer" He put his phone away.

"Guys, my brother has been kidnapped" Michael said panicked.

"Do they know where he is?" Fritz asked.

"No, unfortunately" Michael said then walked

up to Charlie

"Charlie, you need to see if you can find him.

Please, for my sake" Michael begged.

"Ok, I'll try" She replied

Charlie put her hand together, mimicking what Jeremy did in the cell. It worked. She could see everything, the prison, and the buildings next to it. She also saw two guys carrying an unconscious person. They did look similar to Michael.

"Is this him?" Charlie said holding Michael.

Michael stumbled back in shock.

"Y...yeah. It is" Michael replied.

"Well then, we better go get him" said Fritz putting his hand in.

"Well then, let's make a pact" he said smiling.

Chapter 4

"Alright, see you tomorrow guys" Michael said cheerfully as his Dad came to pick him up from school.

"Hey there Mike" His father said. "Have a good day in school?"

"Yeah Dad, guess what! Fritz farted in front of the whole class while our teacher was speaking and the whole class was laughing, it was hilarious!" Michael said laughing.

"Aw, that's great Michael" His Dad said. "Hey, we got to go pick up your sister. She's having a party at my new restaurant"

Michael's eyes lit up. He had been begging his Dad to let him go to the new restaurant for ages but he never did.

Michael spent the time on the way bouncing up and down in anticipation. It was exciting smelling and touching new things that Michael had never done to before.

It was quite a long drive there so Michael's dad put in an audiobook in so Michael wouldn't destroy the car with his excessive happiness.

After what seemed like ages according to Michael they were there.

"Alright Michael, time to get out" His dad said which jolted Michael awake from his sleep.

Michael's dad stepped out of the car and Michael tried to do the same but his backpack got stuck on the seatbelt and Michael had a hard time getting it out.

"Dad, I'm stuck" Michael called out but his Dad just stood there at the entrance not moving a muscle looking empty, like he'd just died except his Dad was still alive.

"Dad?" Michael called out again confused.

"Michael, Michael, MICHAEL, stay in the car don't you dare come out!" His Dad shouted out.

"Dad, what's going on?" Michael asked.

His dad came back his eyes red with tears.

"Dad, where's Ellie?" Michael asked again confused.

Suddenly, his Dad snapped.

"She's dead, ok Michael. She's never coming back, now stop asking me questions and get back into the car NOW!"

The ride back home was sad and silent.

His dad spent the remainder of his time in his room separating himself from the world. He only ever came out to go to the restroom or to have dinner.

Michael didn't mind it until his Mother left. She said to him with teary eyes

"I'll be back in a couple of weeks ok? Look after Dad for me"

One day when his Dad was in the toilet Michael decided to go into his office to investigate.

He quietly walked up the stairs to his dad's room. He silently opened the door and almost puked.

The smell was unidentifiable and there were piles of paper everywhere. He looked over to the table to a folder that said 'my plans' on it. He opened it and gasped.

His dad was the one who was making the children disappear. He looked at the paper that his dad had written on and it said

'I need to do this. I need to help Ellie get better. I need her to be alive.'

Michael could feel tears in his eyes.

He heard footsteps behind him

"WHAT ARE YOU DOING IN MY OFFICE?" It was his dad shouting at him.

His dad walked up to him

"I'm sorry Dad. But answer me please. What are you doing?" Michael said still teary eyed.

"Listen son" His dad knelt down "I'm trying to make Ellie alive again. I've seen it. I know I can do it"

"Then why are kids disappearing?" Michael shouted.

"Because, I heard some kids your age, in your class have special powers that if combined can do anything. I need to get these powers to revive Ellie but that also means unfortunately have to kill them in order to see if they do" His dad replied clearly mad

"Michael, I need you to help me" His Dad said

"Why?" Michael asked

"Because it would be easier if you inspected the kids in your class, then I wouldn't need to kill any of them" His Dad replied

Michael thought about it.

"Ok, then" Said Michael not sure what else to do.

His dad nodded and walked off.

Over the next few days, his dad showed him more and more of what he was doing until he had successfully indoctrinated Michael into believing that what he was doing was right.

"Dad" Michael called

"Yes?" His dad replied.

"My friends have been having dreams about someone telling them that they have the power to save the world"

Suddenly Michael's dad jolted up and looked at Michael

"So, they're the ones I'm after" Michael's dad said with a grin on his face.

"You'd better make sure that Charlie and her friends come to me. What's your plan?"

Michael then told his dad on how he would obtain their powers.

"What's going on here?" Michael turned around

It was Jamie, his brother.

"Trying to save Ellie by obtaining the powers from my friends" Michael said.

"No, you can't be" Jamie said angry." I won't let you"

Jamie pulled up his hands and managed to control the wind to blow his dad's paper all over the floor wiping the ink off them.

"How dare you" His dad shouted.

Jamie turned and ran out the door.

You're both monsters!" He screamed before

running out.

Chapter 5

"This must be the place" Fritz whispered as they all snuck behind a wall.

"Was your brother dealing in anything illegal?" Cassidy asked Michael.

"I don't know, he ran away when I was 13" Michael replied.

Suddenly two figures came out of the shadows.

"Who are you guys?" one of them asked.

"Could say the same to you" said Gabriel putting his hand behind his back to charge his lightning.

"Wait, Michael, is that you?" The guy replied

"Oh, Carl. That must be you then, and you must be Emily" Michael retorted.

"Wait, you know these guys?" Fritz asked.

"Yes, they were my brother's friends"

"You know?" Carl laughed "Jamie used to say some weird stuff about you. Called you a monster but he never said why"

"Why would he call you that?" said Charlie looking at Michael suspiciously.

"Anyway, what are you guys doing here?" Emily asked.

"We came to save him" Jeremy replied cutting Gabriel off before he had a chance to say it.

"Yeah but you don't understand" Emily said.

"Jamie's special. He can control the wind"

Everyone gasped.

"Yes well" Gabriel said. "We can control other things" summoning a lightning ball in his palm.

"So wait Michael, it wasn't you who had powers. It was your brother" said Fritz looking at the others and nodding.

Suddenly, Carl and Emily dropped dead on the floor, a bullet right next to them.

"Oh you guys are so clever aren't you" Michael said putting on a mask.

He ran towards the dark entrance of the warehouse and vanished.

When they entered, they saw Jamie's dead body on the floor.

"Why are you doing this Michael?" Charlie shouted

"You want to know why Charlie? Everything I knew and loved was taken away from me and now I have the option to take it back. I'll bring back my sister and dad and everyone else who died along the way. I'll be a god and no one will be able to stop me. Not even you. So, let's begin" He laughed psychotically.

Charlie, Jeremy and Gabriel were swept to the wall unable to move.

"So, let's take you two on" Michael said to Cassidy and Fritz pulling out a blade.

Chapter 6

"Come on Cassidy, get up" Fritz called sticking his hand out for her to get up.

"I've run out of energy Fritz" Cassidy called blushing.

"Oh well, you're face is turning red. Alright then, let's go for a break then. You want a drink?" Fritz said smiling.

"Yeah, sure" Cassidy said smiling back.

Walking inside Fritz walked over to the cupboards.

"Coffee good?" Fritz asked.

"Yeah sure" Cassidy replied.

Fritz pulled out the coffee and realized it was empty.

"Ah crap, we're out. Want to go out to drink?" Fritz asked.

"Oh um... ok" Cassidy replied.

'Is this a date?' Cassidy thought to herself

'No...No. He just ran out of coffee its fine' she replied

Walking down the street, they arrived at the coffee shop and sat down at a table.

"You'd expect it to be busier" Fritz jokingly said.

Just then, Fritz spotted something out of the corner of his eye.

"Is that Stephanie?" Fritz thought out loud.

"Who?" Cassidy asked.

"Oh, the girl I saved from those guys a while back" Fritz replied.

Stephanie then seemed to recognise Fritz and walked over.

"Oh my god, Fritz I haven't seen you in ages" Stephanie said.

"Yeah. Oh and this is Cassidy" Fritz gestured towards Cassidy.

"Hi I'm Cassidy" Cassidy gestured.

"Ah dang it I need to go to the restroom" Cassidy added.

"Alright then, I'll wait." Fritz said smiling.

As Cassidy made her way she ran into Gabriel and Jeremy.

"Having fun with your date" Gabriel teased.

"Oh shut up" Cassidy jokingly responded lightly punching Gabriel.

Stephanie sat down in Cassidy's seat and began to ask questions.

"So, are you dating her?" She teased.

"What? No!" Fritz responded but then he sighed.

"Listen ok, I do really like Cassidy, the way she laughs, her jokes. Maybe it's because I'm the only one who has ever seen that side of her but I really do like her."

"Well I think that you should just go for it." She said

"You think so?" Fritz asked.

"If it works, Cassidy will be very lucky"

Chapter 7

"Cassidy NOW!" Fritz shouted.

Cassidy put her hands to the ground and summoned a gigantic wave. Fritz then jumped onto the wave and started firing fire at Michael.

"No, No, NO!" Michael shrieked. He tried to throw gusts of wind at Cassidy but missed as Fritz kept firing fireballs at him.

Finally, Michael managed to get to Cassidy and kicked her away causing the wave under Fritz's feet to disappear.

"NO!" Charlie shrieked.

"Be QUIET!" Michael shouted back.

Michael started walking over to Cassidy with his blade in hand.

'No' Fritz thought. 'I've spent my whole life trying to ignore my own problems, my flaws. I tormented Cassidy so many times when we were younger because I thought I was helping her. Maybe I'm the reason she's so shy? But, if I'm going to go out it might as well be by protecting the one I love'

Michael went to swing at Cassidy. He closed his eyes, shedding a tear and stopped.

'Had he done it?' he thought.

Opening his eyes he saw not Cassidy but Fritz, smiling with blade in his stomach.

"So, you thought you could hurt Cassidy did you?" Fritz said clearly in pain, stumbling.

"I'm sorry" Michael said crying. He held his hand up and absorbed all of Fritz's power and drew the sword away from Fritz's stomach. Fritz fell.

Michael then walked up to Cassidy and absorbed her power as well.

"Cassidy!" Fritz said weak.

"Before we die. There is something I need to tell you. I'm sorry. I'm sorry for teasing you so many times, about your shyness, about your fears that I should have been sympathetic towards, and I know that this is stupid but Cassidy there's something else I need to tell you. Cassidy, I love you" Fritz said tearing up and closing his eyes.

He felt a pair of hands grab onto his. They were warm and soft. He opened his eyes again and they were Cassidy's.

"It's ok, Fritz. I forgive you. In fact, I forgave you years ago. Also, I love you too. If there's anyone I want to spend my last moments with. It's you."

Slowly, they both held each other's hands and closed their eyes.

Chapter 8

'This is so boring' Gabriel thought as they sat in class. 'Mr Shortland won't stop going on about poems and books'

"Gabriel, can you share with us what you got for the answer?" His teacher called him out.

'Huh' Gabriel thought. 'Wait, I didn't do the work. CRAP! What do I do?'

Suddenly, he felt a nudge at his side. It was Charlie.

"The answer is Wilfred Owen" Charlie whispered.

"Wilfred Owen" Gabriel then called out.

"Yes. Correct" Mr Shortland replied glaring slightly at Charlie.

'Jeez that was a drag' Gabriel thought as he headed out the classroom for lunch.

"Oh, thanks Charlie for saving my ass there" Gabriel said laughing.

"Don't thank me, thank Jeremy. He asked me to tell you that since he was too far away" Charlie replied.

"OK then, thanks Jeremy." He said as Jeremy walked past.

"Anyway, I and the others are going to get lunch, you want to come with?" Charlie asked.

"I would but Jeremy and I have packed lunches today so we can't sorry." Gabriel replied.

"Oh ok, Have fun on your date!" Charlie said laughing.

"Ha-ha, very funny" Gabriel replied, "Come on Jeremy, let's go."

There Gabriel and Jeremy were discussing random stuff.

"So, I saw this video by someone called Koomaxx. So, kiss, marry, and kill Mineta, Shiguraki, and Nomu." Jeremy asked.

"Oh, that is a hard one. I'll go-"Gabriel was cut off.

"Um... hi Gabriel. I was wondering if you wanted to go out sometime." She could see Gabriel's confused face. "Like on a date" She corrected.

Gabriel realizing what he was being asked stumbled back in surprise.

'Why is he stumbling? He gets this all the time' Jeremy thought then rolled his eyes.

"Well, sorry I'm not ready for a date I mean I'm still in school." Gabriel replied.

Gabriel was surprised when the girl started shouting back.

"What, are you too good for me? Well you don't even deserve one! Have fun with your boyfriend over there!" She stormed off before Gabriel responded.

"Listen, you can insult me all you want, you can say that I don't deserve a girlfriend, you can say anything bad about me that you like but one thing that I will never let you do is insult Jeremy or any other one of my friends. Jeremy has always been there for me. He's one of the only people to not be my friend for my popularity but because he thinks I'm a good person. I don't even care that he's egotistical, at least he's there for me." Gabriel replied in a quiet and direct voice.

The girl stormed off leaving Jeremy and Gabriel there to wait until lunch was over.

Chapter 9

"Now!" Charlie yelled as she, Gabriel and Jeremy charged full speed into Michael as he was distracted dealing with Cassidy and Fritz.

Pinning him up against the wall, Jeremy and Gabriel changed their limbs to that of lightning and wood and started punching and kicking Michael.

"No, I won't go down yet, I'll kill you just like I killed Cassidy, Fritz, all your parents and siblings and Susie.

After hearing that Jeremy, Gabriel and Charlie stumbled back in shock.

"What?" Charlie shook.

"Yes, it was me who killed Susie. I needed a reason to bring you all together and I didn't want your parents getting in the way so I killed them!" Michael was going insane. "To top it all off it was my father who killed the kids in the bunny costume at the restaurant."

Charlie was reminded of how odd Michael's father looked when they were there.

"Why though? Why did you kill everyone? What did they do?" Jeremy shouted which made Gabriel shocked because Jeremy hadn't shown much emotion in ages.

"It was to bring back my sister. She died in one of dad's restaurants and he never forgave himself so he decided to look for the people with powers that would make him a god to bring back Ellie. However…" Michael looked down. "He died before he could get his hands on you. I told him my plan to get you all here when you were older because then it'd be easier but he didn't listen. I may not be able to fully revive my dad but I do have enough to bring him back as a husk. He won't be human but he'll still have emotions."

With that, Michael put his hands together and suddenly a creature appeared baring resemblance to Michael's dad.

"Well done my son" His Father jerked.

Suddenly his father started running in a jerky manner towards Gabriel.

'What's going on? Why is this happening? This isn't Michael. Is it?' Gabriel thought as he was ready to die. He looked up confused as to why he wasn't dead yet. There was Jeremy in front of him facing Michael's dad.

"You know what?" Jeremy said coughing blood. "I don't think you ever thanked Michael's dad for letting you spend your party at his house instead of yours because your parents were divorcing, but I guess that doesn't matter now since he's now just a mindless killer." He turned to Michael's dad.

"We will never forgive you for turning Michael against us!" He shouted pushing Michael's dad away then falling to the floor.

"I didn't want to do this." Michael shouted crying walking over to Gabriel and Jeremy. "You made me. You could've talked to me or anything but no you left me to grieve. You didn't care how I felt so I shouldn't care how you feel but I still do."

"Michael, do you think this would make Ellie happy. Why would she want you becoming a serial killer?" Charlie asked.

"I'll revive everyone when I'm done. Then I won't be a serial killer."

"But what about all the people your dad killed before figuring out we were the ones with powers?" Charlie asked again with tears in her eyes.

"That doesn't matter. It was ages ago. It will all be worth it I know it!" Michael answered shouting and crying.

"Is this what Ellie would have wanted? To see you kill all your friends just so she could live?" Gabriel shouted.

Michael stumbled back not knowing how to answer.

"Oh, you're a weak child." Michael's dad hissed before running up to Gabriel and stabbing him.

Both Gabriel and Jeremy fell to the floor.

To both of them, it was all a blur. They weren't thinking of the action going on around them, they were thinking of each other.

"I would kill Mineta, kiss Nomu and marry Shiguraki!" Gabriel stuttered.

"What?" Jeremy replied chuckling.

"Remember, the question you asked me in middle school." Gabriel answered.

"Oh, right" Jeremy said.

'If I could go back and do over the things that happened in those years I would.' Gabriel and Jeremy said in unison as they closed their eyes watching the action that was happening elsewhere.

Chapter 10

Absorbing Gabriel and Jeremy's powers Michael then started walking over to Charlie.

"No give me yours or else!" Michael said trapping Charlie in tree bark.

Just then, Charlie heard a voice.

"Charlie, it's me, Ellie, use your powers to send me to Michael." Charlie didn't know what to do but as if by magic her body reacted and sent Ellie to Michael.

Michael stumbled back into a place that he didn't recognise. It was a mixture of all different colours and the ground was non-existent but he could still stand. Looking up, he gasped. There was Ellie sitting looking over at him.

"E...Ellie?" Michael stuttered running over.

Ellie stopped him before he could hug her. She slapped him with tears in her eyes.

"Who are you?" She asked him.

"What? It's me Michael." He replied confused.

"No, I don't think it is. The real Michael wouldn't do any of this. The real Michael wouldn't kill any of his friends just so I could live. The real Michael would stay strong even when sad. However, if the real Michael now killed his friends so I could live then I don't want to live." She replied.

"Yeah but, I'm going to revive them with my powers when it's done just like how I'll revive you. Then we can all be friends again." Michael said.

"Yes, but what's done is done. It doesn't matter whether you can revive them you still killed them. I don't want to live in a world where you're a killer Michael." She said teary eyed hugging Michael.

It hit Michael. Everything he had ever done, killed Susie, Fritz, Cassidy, Gabriel and Jeremy and soon Charlie. He had killed all their parents so that he could steal their powers easier. He had let everyone he knew down. He knew what he had to do.

"You're right. Who am I now?" He questioned.

"Don't worry Ellie, I'll bring back the real Michael."

"You'd better!" Ellie said laughing.

With that, Michael was back to the real world.

Michael looked over at his dad.

"I'll kill you Charlie!" His dad shouted running full speed at her.

'No.' Michael thought. 'I need to stop my father and save Charlie.'

Michael ran to combat his father but was too late so he put his hand out in front of Charlie to protect her.

Michael used all his friends' powers to kill his father.

"NO, you traitor!" His father yelled as he crumbled away into dust.

Michael fell to the floor defenceless releasing Charlie who then ran over to Michael.

"Charlie, you can hate me if you want. To be honest right now I don't view myself that highly." Michael chuckled then started crying.

"No, I don't. I could never hate you." She hugged him.

Michael then put his hands together and in his last breath revived everyone.

Fritz, Cassidy and Gabriel and Jeremy woke up
to find their powers had come back to them.

"So," Fritz began. "You said you loved me
Cassidy."

"I do!" She replied as they went and kissed.

Epilogue

"Fritz, wake up!" Gabriel shouted.

Fritz woke up with a jolt.

"Man, you really are impossible sometimes."
Gabriel laughed.

"You told me we would be late." Fritz shouted.

"Well I lied, but it got you out of bed and also
I'm an early bird and you should be early as it's
your wedding day." Gabriel responded.

"Fine then. I made sure not to drink too much
unlike this guy over here." He said pointing at
Jeremy who was still asleep.

"Hey, you wanted to make it a special day so you didn't even drink at all." Gabriel chuckled.

"Hey, you didn't either. Besides, I don't want Cassidy to think I'm a bad husband already do I." Fritz responded jokingly.

"Yeah but turns out I'm allergic to alcohol. I can't say the same for Jeremy so wake up Buddy." He directed that to Jeremy.

Jeremy woke up with a jolt.

"Alright then, we're all up time to get ready." Gabriel said.

After the ceremony, Charlie decided to wander around a little. Looking at everyone there made her feel really happy. Fritz and Cassidy were talking to their old teachers and Gabriel and Jeremy seemed to be making passive aggressive comments about each other.

"So, it's all over. I wonder what's left in store for me." Charlie said to Fritz.

"So what do you think you're going to do now?" Fritz asked.

"I think I'm going to start a new life by myself. I'll distance myself as much as possible from my house and that restaurant. You have fun Fritz and Cassidy. " Charlie replied.

"Don't forget to visit us sometime." Cassidy chuckled.

"Don't worry I will." Charlie said.

As she left she swore she could see all of

Michael's family and him waving at her. Charlie

smiled. After Michael's sacrifice, she knew that

a wave back wouldn't cause any harm. It was

time for them to forget their pasts, and

embrace the new lives ahead of them.

Printed in Great Britain
by Amazon

45015147R00052